FREEDOM FORCES

★ U.S. ARMY: ★

GROUND ASSAULT

Carla Mooney

Rourke
Educational Media
rourkeeducationalmedia.com

Scan for Related Titles and
Teacher Resources

www.rourkeeducationalmedia.com

PHOTO CREDITS: Cover and title page metal border © Eky Studio, cover photo courtesy U.S. Army; back cover and title page: flag © SFerdon; Pages 4/5 courtesy US Military, US Air Force; Page courtesy U.S. Army; Page 7 © Skryl Sergey; Pages 8/9 © National Archives and Records Administration, William B. T. Trego, US Military, US Army; Pages 10/11 courtesy US Army; Pages 12/13 © US Army, Elizabeth M. Lorge, David Dismukes, Glenn Fawcett; Pages 14 © John Davis, Mike A. Glasch, Fort Jackson Leader; Pages 15 © US Army, US Air Force, Spc. Daniel Scneider 366th MPAD, USD-C; Pages 16/17 © Sgt. Timothy Kingston, US Army, Joseph A. Lambach U.S. Marine Corps, SGT Igor Paustovski, US Army, U.S. Department of Defense, US Army; Pages 18/19 © US Army, Sgt. Andy Dunaway US Army, Staff Sgt. Samuel Bendet US Air Force, SGT Tom Pullin; Pages 20/21 © Photographer's Mate 2nd Class Daniel J. McLain US Navy, Spc. James B. Smith Jr. US Army, US Navy, Ultratone85, US Army, US Air Force; Pages 22/23 © Spc. Michael J. MacLeod US Army, US Army, Jennifer Andersson; Pages 24/25 © Gary A. Bryant US Army, Spc. Ryan Hallock, Pfc. Kim, Jun-sub; Pages 26/27 © US Army, US Air Force, US Military; Pages 28/29 © National Archives and Records Administration and U.S. Army

Edited by Precious McKenzie

Designed and Produced by Blue Door Publishing, FL

Library of Congress Cataloging-in-Publication Data

Carla Mooney U.S. Army: Ground Assault
  p. cm. -- (Freedom Forces)
  ISBN 978-1-62169-921-7 (hard cover) (alk. paper)
  ISBN 978-1-62169-816-6 (soft cover)
  ISBN 978-162717-025-3 (e-book)
  Library of Congress Control Number: 2013938873

Rourke Educational Media
Printed in the United States of America,
North Mankato, Minnesota

Also Available as:
ROURKE'S
e-Books

Rourke
Educational Media

rourkeeducationalmedia.com
customerservice@rourkeeducationalmedia.com
PO Box 643328 Vero Beach, Florida 32964

TABLE OF CONTENTS

CHAPTER ONE GROUND ATTACK

When facing a fierce enemy, who are the first forces sent into **combat**? Army soldiers lead the ground attack. Army soldiers fire weapons, launch **missiles**, and operate **radar**. Army officers lead the troops and make crucial battlefield decisions.

U.S. soldiers wear protective clothing and carry their equipment with them.

The Army is the largest branch of the United States Armed Forces. Other branches of the Armed Forces are the Marine Corps, the Navy, the Air Force, and the Coast Guard. The Army is in charge of all land warfare. Army soldiers may also perform **humanitarian** and **peacekeeping** duties.

U.S. Humanitarian Assistance insures that food and other vital supplies reach populations in need after a war or large-scale emergency.

The U.S. Army is one of the largest and most powerful in the entire world. It has more than 488,000 active duty soldiers. The Army also has about 189,000 Reserve soldiers. Reserve soldiers are called to duty when needed during a national emergency or global conflict.

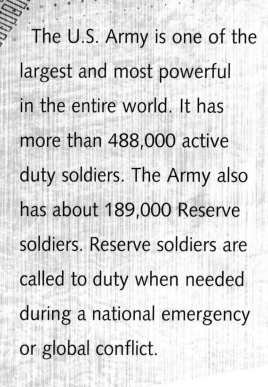

Army Structure

Corps
20,000 to 45,000 soldiers

Division
10,000 to 15,000 soldiers

Brigade
3,000 to 5,000 soldiers

Battalion
300 to 5,000 soldiers

Company
62 to 190 soldiers

Platoon
16 to 44 soldiers

Squad
9 to 10 soldiers

Because the Army is so large, it is organized into units.

Soldier's Rank Insignias

General

Lieutenant General

Major General

Colonel

Lieutenant Colonel

Captain

Lieutenant

Staff Sergeant

CHAPTER TWO

ARMY HISTORY

How did the U.S. Army get started? The Army can trace its history all the way back to the founding of America. The Continental Congress founded the Army on June 14, 1775. It was called the Continental Army. General George Washington led the Army against the British in the American Revolution. Since then, the Army has fought in wars around the world.

George Washington and Continental Army at Long Island in New York.

U.S. Army soldiers engage enemy forces during Operation Moshtarak in Badula Qulp, Afghanistan.

U.S. Army soldiers during Operation MacArthur in the Vietnam War.

Army soldiers battled for America in the War of 1812, the Mexican War, the Civil War, and World Wars I and II. They fought in Vietnam's jungles and the deserts of Iraq and Afghanistan.

Today, the Army's main job is to defend and protect the United States and its freedoms at home and around the world. To do this, the Army has strategic bases worldwide.

ARMY POSTS IN OTHER COUNTRIES

★ = ARMY POST

The U.S. Rangers were first used on the American frontier in 1670. They were expert riflemen in the American Revolution. In the Civil War, Rangers fought on both sides, for the North and for the South. They fought in World War II. Rangers served in Korea, Vietnam, Afghanistan, and Iraq.

U.S. Army Rangers

The 75th Ranger Regiment is known as the U.S. Army Rangers. It is a flexible, highly trained, light **infantry** force. The Rangers can be sent anywhere in the world within 18 hours. They are known worldwide for their toughness.

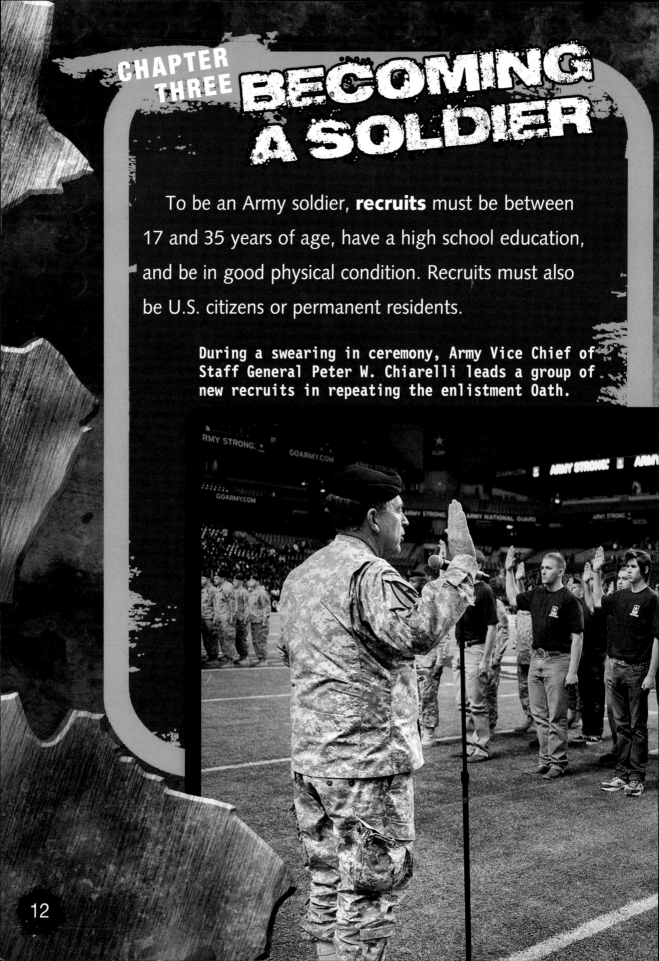

CHAPTER THREE

BECOMING A SOLDIER

To be an Army soldier, **recruits** must be between 17 and 35 years of age, have a high school education, and be in good physical condition. Recruits must also be U.S. citizens or permanent residents.

During a swearing in ceremony, Army Vice Chief of Staff General Peter W. Chiarelli leads a group of new recruits in repeating the enlistment Oath.

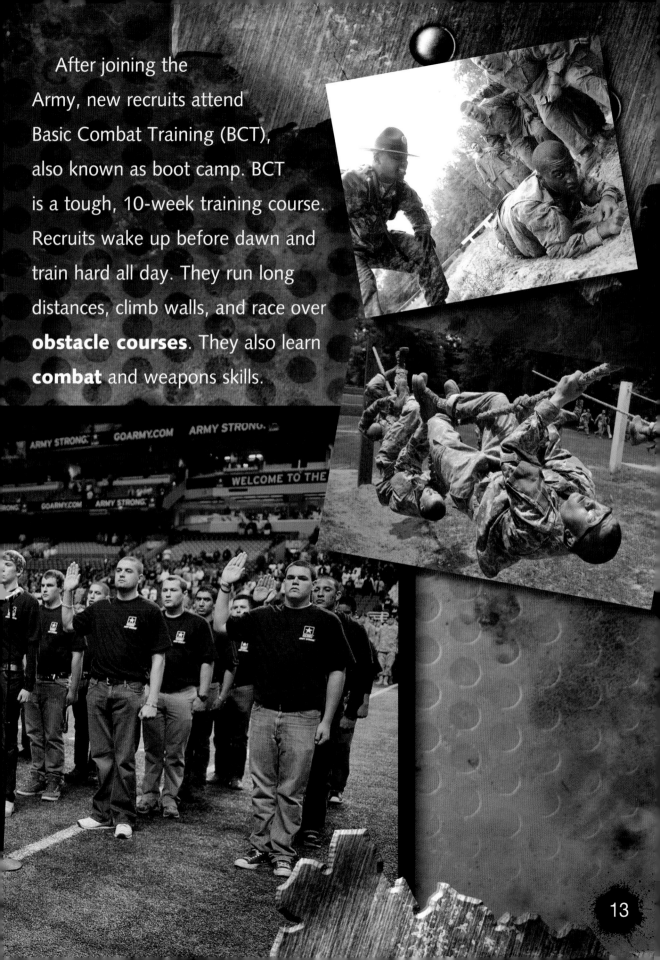

After joining the Army, new recruits attend Basic Combat Training (BCT), also known as boot camp. BCT is a tough, 10-week training course. Recruits wake up before dawn and train hard all day. They run long distances, climb walls, and race over **obstacle courses**. They also learn **combat** and weapons skills.

13

After Basic Combat Training, soldiers go to Advanced Individual Training (AIT). They receive hands-on training and field instruction to learn the skills they will need for their Army jobs.

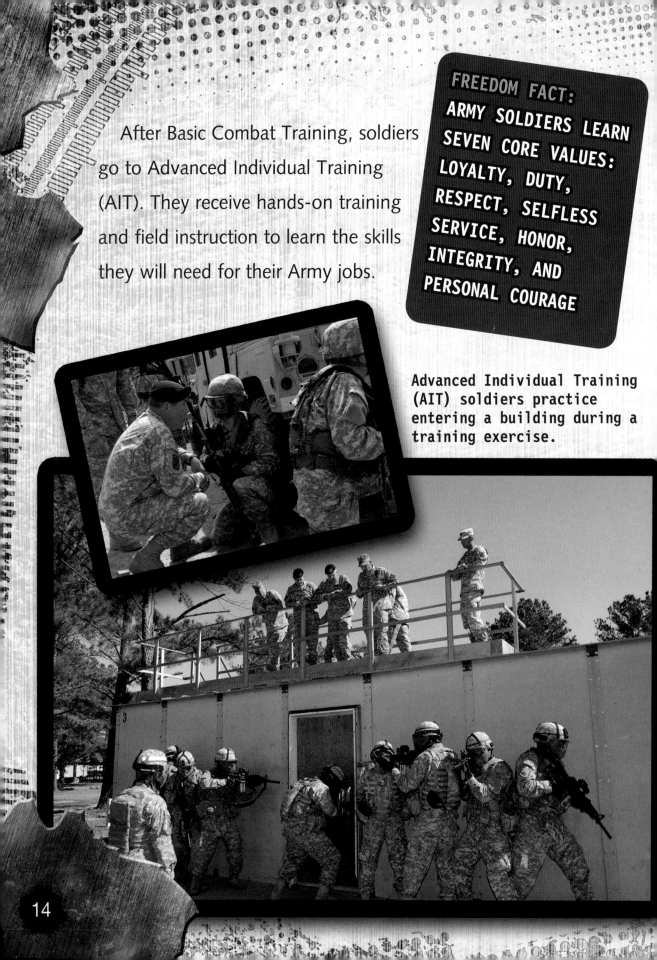

Advanced Individual Training (AIT) soldiers practice entering a building during a training exercise.

There are more than 150 different Army jobs. Soldiers may learn advanced infantry skills, how to operate high-tech missile systems, or maintain weaponry systems. They may choose jobs in areas such as medicine, science, technology, engineering, and construction. All of these jobs are needed to make the Army run smoothly.

The U.S. Army's Green Berets are trained for special operations around the world. The Green Berets stop acts of terrorism. They gather information and destroy enemy weapons. Some missions recover people or spy on enemies. Sometimes the Green Berets assist forces deep in enemy territory.

THE ARMY OFFERS CAREERS IN A HUGE VARIETY OF FIELDS. HERE ARE SOME OF THE MOST POPULAR:

★ financial manager
★ interpreter
★ intelligence analyst
★ graphic designer
★ military police
★ artillery specialist
★ satellite communications systems operator
★ dental specialist
★ aircraft electronics

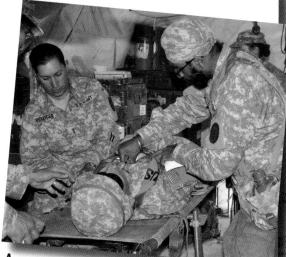

Army soldiers performing and perfecting their tactics for both combat and training scenarios.

Here is a website to find more info on careers
http://www.goarmy.com/careers-and-jobs/browse-career-and-job-categories.html

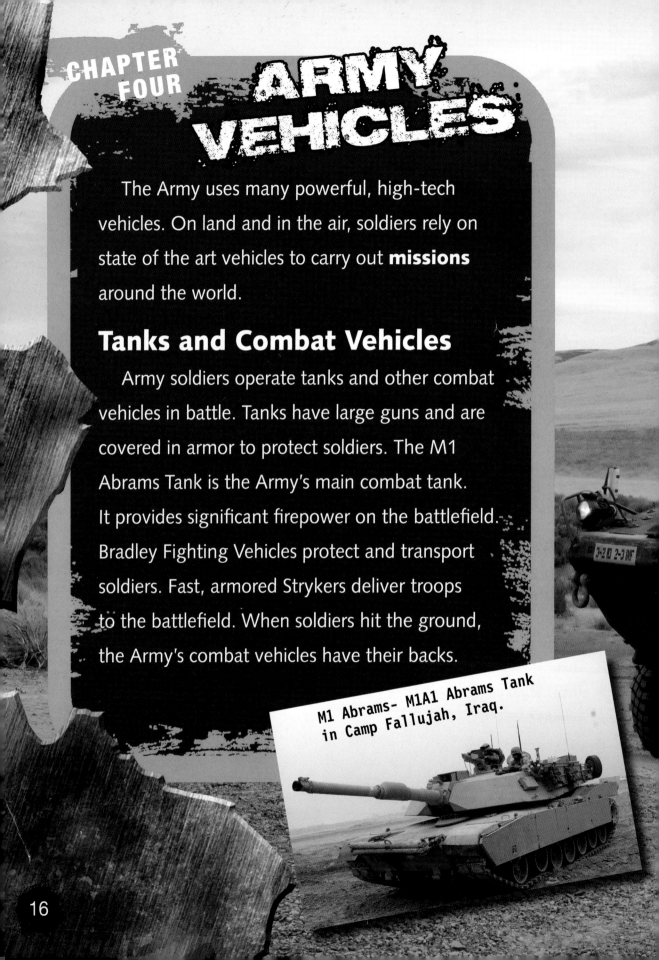

ARMY VEHICLES

The Army uses many powerful, high-tech vehicles. On land and in the air, soldiers rely on state of the art vehicles to carry out **missions** around the world.

Tanks and Combat Vehicles

Army soldiers operate tanks and other combat vehicles in battle. Tanks have large guns and are covered in armor to protect soldiers. The M1 Abrams Tank is the Army's main combat tank. It provides significant firepower on the battlefield. Bradley Fighting Vehicles protect and transport soldiers. Fast, armored Strykers deliver troops to the battlefield. When soldiers hit the ground, the Army's combat vehicles have their backs.

M1 Abrams- M1A1 Abrams Tank in Camp Fallujah, Iraq.

Bradley Fighting Vehicle

A Stryker gunnery on a training mission.

Helicopters

Army helicopters can be part of air assaults, spy on enemies, transport troops, and carry supplies.

The AH-64 Apache Longbow is the Army's main attack helicopter. It carries missiles and other weapons. It can fly during the day or at night in all weather conditions.

The UH-60 Black Hawk transports troops. It is also used for air assaults and medical missions.

AH-64D Apache Longbow

The four bladed, twin engine utility helicopter known as the UH-60 Black Hawk participated in the largest air assault mission in U.S. Army history in 1991.

UAVs

The latest and most secretive of all military vehicles are Unmanned Aerial Vehicles (UAVs), or drones. UAVs fly without a pilot on board. They are controlled remotely by pilots from the ground. UAVs can fly into areas that are too dangerous for pilots, such as those contaminated by chemical or biological weapons. UAVs can spy on enemies or drop bombs while keeping soldiers safely at a distance.

MQ-9 Reaper

Shadow 200 UAV

Aerial demonstrators at the 2005 Naval Unmanned Aerial Vehicle Air Demo held at the Webster Field Annex of Naval Air Station Patuxent River.

Support Vehicles

Other support vehicles assist soldiers on a variety of missions. The Humvee travels over difficult terrain. It carries troops, weapons, and shelters. The Humvee can also be used as an ambulance, missile carrier, or scout vehicle. Heavy expanded mobility tactical trucks (HEMTTs) are used to re-supply combat vehicles and weapons systems. They can be used in all weather conditions. The M1070 heavy equipment transport (HET) vehicle can haul the heaviest battle tanks. These vehicles are some of the strongest and most maneuverable in the world.

Humvee

The diesel-electric HEMTT A3 uses a 20mm M61A1 Gatling gun that fires M-940 rounds at a rate of 4,500 shots per minute.

HIGH-TECH WEAPONS AND GEAR

Army soldiers use some of the most high-tech gear and weapons in the world. GPS (Global Positioning System) Locators use satellites to find a precise location and figure out how close soldiers are to their units and targets.

U.S. Army 2nd Lt. Corey Luffler, platoon leader and Spc. Joseph Hebert determine a GPS grid coordinate.

Ghillie suits cover soldiers from head to toe in synthetic vegetation to conceal them during top secret missions.

Soldiers wear night-vision goggles to see targets in the dark. The goggles collect tiny amounts of light that are present but the naked eye cannot see and **amplifies** them. This allows the wearer to easily see images even in the dark.

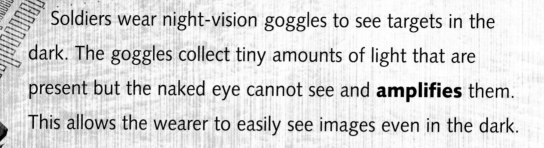

FREEDOM FACT:
GREEN TECHNOLOGY LESSENS THE ARMY'S DEPENDENCE ON FUEL. SOLAR PANELS ON TENTS CAN RUN POWER LIGHTS AND SEVERAL COMPUTERS.

Remote-controlled robots carry heavy equipment and explore dangerous areas. By using robots instead of humans, the Army hopes to protect their soldiers.

Talon robots are designed to perform missions ranging from reconnaissance to combat and operate in a number of hostile environments.

Army soldiers also use powerful weapons. They fire assault rifles, machine guns, and sniper rifles in combat. The M-16 rifle is a general assault weapon. The M4 Carbine is a semiautomatic gun with a short barrel that works in tight spaces. Army soldiers are highly trained in safety and accuracy.

The U.S. Army is highly trained and powerful. It uses some of the most high-tech weapons, gear, and vehicles available. The Army's brave soldiers fight to protect America's freedom around the world.

The M240 Machine Gun can fire 200 to 600 rounds per minute with barrels hot enough to inflict second degree burns instantly.

TIMELINE

1775:
U.S. Army formed.

1783:
Army defeats Great Britain in American Revolution.

1802:
Congress establishes the U.S. Military Academy at West Point, New York.

1898:
Spanish-American War.

1917:
The U.S. enters World War I.

1941:
The U.S. enters World War II.

1965-1973:
Vietnam War.

1991:
Operation Desert Storm begins the first Persian Gulf War.

2001:
Invasion of Afghanistan.

1812-1815:

The Army fights Great Britain in the War of 1812.

1846-1848:

Mexican-American War.

1861-1865:

Civil War.

1944:

The Allies invade Western Europe on D-Day, June 6th.

1945:

World War II ends.

1950-1953:

The Korean War.

2003:

The U.S. Army leads invasion of Iraq.

SHOW WHAT YOU KNOW

1. When was the U.S. Army founded?
2. About how many soldiers serve in the U.S. Army?
3. What is the first training course new Army recruits take?
4. What foreign countries have U.S. Army bases?
5. What are the requirements to join the Army?

GLOSSARY

amplifies (AM-pluh-fahyz): to make larger, greater, or stronger

combat (KOM-bat): armed fighting with enemy forces

humanitarian (hyoo-man-i-TAIR-ee-uhn): having concern for and helping to ease the suffering of people

infantry (in-FUHN-tree): ground troops

missiles (MISS-uhlz): explosive weapons that can travel long distances

missions (MISH-uhns): military tasks

obstacle courses (OB-stuh-kuhl KORSS-iz): a series of barriers that soldiers must jump over, climb, or crawl through

peacekeeping (PEES-kee-ping): military activities to prevent further fighting between countries or groups of people

radar (RAY-dar): a device that uses radio waves to track the location of objects

recruits (ri-KROOTS): members of the armed forces

Index

Websites to Visit

http://www.goarmy.com/about.html

http://www.army.mil/join/

http://www.u-s-history.com/pages/h1963.html

About the Author

Carla Mooney has written many books for children
and young adults. She lives in Pennsylvania with
her husband and three children. She enjoys learning
about U.S. history and reading stories of Army
soldiers in past battles.

Meet The Author!
www.rem4students.com

32